INSTAFAMOUS

EVAN JACOBS

SADDLEBACK
EDUCATIONAL PUBLISHING

MONARCH JUNGLE

SADDLEBACK
EDUCATIONAL PUBLISHING
www.sdlback.com

ISBN-13: 978-1-68021-477-2
ISBN-10: 1-68021-477-2
eBook: 978-1-63078-831-5

Printed in Guangzhou, China
NOR/1117/CA21701345

22 21 20 19 18   1 2 3 4 5

MONARCH
JUNGLE

BEING KEVIN SANDERS

Kevin Sanders!" people shouted. "I love your videos!"

"Make sure to like and comment," Kevin said. He pushed his hair back and smiled.

Fans held up their phones. He posed for photos.

"Let's go," a man said. He was Kevin's helper. Right now he had one job. Get the star through the crowd.

A path had been roped off. But some fans ducked under it.

"Back!" the man yelled.

"Pipeline," Kevin called. "Come to the booth." He held up his phone. Fans cheered.

Hollywood had film stars. These were online stars. There were dancers and singers. Some wrote books. Others were bloggers. Many stars gave tips. They were about fashion and makeup.

Their posts got millions of views. It was how regular people got famous. There was a name for it. Instafamous.

Take Kevin. He did pranks. Millions loved his YouTube videos. When he wasn't posting, he was at events. Meeting fans was important.

Today he was at See It Live. It was held once a year in LA. Tickets sold out in minutes. If you were here, you'd made it.

Fans were a big part. But it was also about business. Agents handled that. They made deals. Companies paid stars to use their products. That was how Kevin teamed up with Pipeline Clothing.

They saw a video he made. He was surfing with a shark. Then the video went viral. The company wanted a deal. Three million people followed Kevin on Instagram. One photo of him sold tons of stuff. In this case, it was surf gear.

Kevin made money too. He got four grand to be here. His agent set it up. Ron Simon made great deals. Today the deal was simple. Wear the clothes and pose for selfies.

"Kevin Sanders!" a woman called out. She was a reporter. "What are you working on?"

"Aww. You know I can't say." He gave her a sly grin. "It'll ruin the surprise."

He was working on a show for YouTube. It was called "I Am Kevin Sanders."

"Come on, Kev," she said. "Tell us."

"Yeah, Kev," a voice said. "We want to know."

It was Chase Rogers. He was also an online star. Sometimes the two teamed up for pranks.

"What's up?" Kevin said.

"Your shirt," Chase said.

"What about it?"

"It's Pipeline's. They hired me! You're a cheap fake!"

"Don't make me hurt you," Kevin said. He gave Chase a push. Suddenly the crowd rushed in. They started to pull the guys apart. But the two had stepped aside. People hadn't seen them. Now the crowd turned on each other.

Kevin headed for the exit. At the door, he looked back. A fight had broken out. Chase was close behind. They each ran to a limo and got in. Kevin called Chase.

"That was epic!" Kevin said.

"Dude!" Chase said. "Check out YouTube. This thing is blowing up! The traffic's on fire!"

"Doesn't take much, does it?"

"Are you kidding? We started a riot."

Chapter 2

COMMITTED

The limo stopped at Kevin's house. He lived with his parents in LA. Some called his family rich.

"Hi," Kevin said when he walked in. His parents were online working. Kevin's career was a full-time job. The money he made had paid for their home.

"You guys are online more than me."

His dad didn't look up. "That prank with Chase? Over one million views."

"I know," Kevin said. "That's up from a minute ago."

"Checking Instagram now," his mom said. "You have more followers."

"Cool," Kevin said. He loved his parents. And they had to love him. He was their son. But at times he wondered. Was it about love? Or was it the money?

"Good news," Kevin's dad said. "You're booked for the month. Want to hear the schedule?"

Do I have a choice?

"Be Seen photo shoot. True Stars meet and greet. The Show List event in—"

"Hold on," Kevin said. "I have a test in two weeks. When will I study?"

"Dad spoke to your teacher," Kevin's mom said. "You can make it up."

Kevin looked at his dad. "Are you sure it was the right teacher? Mr. Fail-'Em-All Foster?"

"Yep. His son follows you. He thinks you're … How did he put it? Oh yeah. Da bomb."

His mom looked up. "You know the deal. Five days for school. Weekends are for work. No rest for the famous."

Sometimes Kevin felt like he was being pranked. He just wanted to be normal. But what was normal?

"See you later," he said. Kevin stood at the door, watching them. They never looked up.

Kevin's phone buzzed. It was a text from his girlfriend.

"Don't forget. We're meeting at the mall."

Being around Kyla made Kevin feel calm. Was that how normal felt? Whatever it was, it worked.

The two had met when they were juniors. Kevin couldn't help but notice her. She was so tall. Later he found out she played basketball. He started going to the games.

Finally Kevin asked her out. They talked the whole time. He liked how smart she was. It was good to be with someone on his level. But Kyla wasn't his type. Not because she was smart. Because of her online status.

Kyla had only a small following. It wasn't something she worked at. But somehow they stayed together. Deep down he knew the reason. He needed an escape. It's what kept him from going insane.

Now they walked through the mall holding hands.

"Sorry I wasn't at See It Live," Kyla said. "I know it was a big deal for you."

"You could've come," he said. "There was room in my limo."

"Ha-ha." She leaned over and nudged him. "Not all of us can be stars. Some of us have to study."

"What can I say? I rule. You could be a star too. You just need millions of followers. Like me."

"I guess. But why? It's not real."

"That reminds me of Bryan," Kevin said.

Bryan Lowe and Kevin used to be partners. They had a channel on YouTube. It was called "Lowe and Lower." They did basic pranks, like wear masks and scare people. Or they'd make gross noises in public places. Anything to get a reaction.

The two also had a show. It was called "Pop-up Pranks." They'd go random places and give classes. Once it was karate. Another time yoga. It wasn't real. But they always got laughs.

Then it all changed. Kevin didn't know it at the time. He found out later. Bryan had been feeling stress. It wasn't the pranks. It was Instagram. Keeping up with it was a lot of work. But Bryan pushed himself harder.

It became an endless loop. Taking photos and editing them. At night, he'd scroll his feed rather than sleep. He'd stay up tracking likes and comments. He'd even check the number of double taps. That showed his fans really loved him.

Finally it got to be too much. Bryan got sick. It was some kind of meltdown. His mom had a word for it. *Agoraphobia.* It was a fear of going places.

Kevin didn't know how to help. So he stayed away. A year had gone by since then.

Chapter 3

BORED

Huge sneaker deal in the works!" It was a text from Kevin's agent.

"Keep them coming," Kevin texted back.

"Put the phone away!" Mr. Harris yelled. He was the sub for English. Kids called him Heartless Harris behind his back. The man was not nice.

"Lighten up," Kevin said. "I'm doing work." It was true. It just wasn't schoolwork.

Mr. Harris pointed at Kevin's phone. "I'll take it."

"Relax," Kevin said. He put the phone into his pocket.

"Okay, class," the teacher said. "You have the assignment. Ms. Ward wants it done by Friday."

The class had been reading a book. It was called *The Catcher in the Rye*. Today students were working in groups. They had to define words they didn't know.

Kevin typed *blasé* into the search box. *Having no interest in something.* So sad but so true.

Being a video star helped at times like this. Kevin knew how to act. Now he sat up straight. He nodded as kids talked.

Mr. Harris seemed to buy it. He turned to face the board. Kevin took out his phone. He'd have to text fast. At one point, he looked up. Harris had reached behind his back.

Something made Kevin start filming. Harris slid his hand into his back pocket. Then he took it out. This was too good. Kevin did a quick edit.

After class, he uploaded the video. One of his friends came up. It was Adam. "Check this out," Kevin said.

The video was on Instagram. Harris moved his hand up and down. It looked like he was scratching his rear-end. There was a caption with it. "What is this sub teaching us? #nobuttsaboutit." It was already trending.

"This is killer, dude!" Adam said. "You got his good side."

Nick walked up to them. He was another friend of Kevin's. "I'm dying here," he said. "This is a Paulson High first."

Adam looked at Nick. "Kev doesn't care about that. He's already famous. Right, Kev?"

Kevin nodded as he tapped the view count. It was up from a second ago.

"Kev does it like a boss," Adam said. "He's making mad bank."

These kids hadn't always hung out with Kevin. In fact, they didn't know each other at first. They had little in common. Adam wore tank tops and flip-flops, even in winter. And Nick was a rich kid into designer labels.

Kevin had been taking drama. He wasn't into social media then. It was his acting teacher who brought it up. "If you want to act, you need to be online." Kevin took the advice.

Soon he had a small following. It was mostly kids at school. Some started hanging around Kevin. Adam and Nick were two of them. They thought he was cool. Kevin had a different idea. He thought they wanted a piece of the fame.

That gave him an idea. He reached out on Instagram. "Follow me @KevinSanders. I'll follow you back." It worked. Kevin's attention was worth something.

After that he posted every day. It would be a picture of him. Or it was something he liked. He spent time on the photos. They had to be perfect. He used filters to make them pop. His captions were clever. Then his numbers jumped.

Who needed drama class? Kevin was famous. He just had to keep his fans happy.

"Hey," Nick said. "I just got a text. It's about Mr. Harris. He quit."

"What?" Kevin looked up from his phone.

"Yeah. It was your video." Nick was reading from the text. "Kids wouldn't stop watching it. Harris walked out."

Chapter 4

LOSING FACE

Kevin had lost interest in the football game. He was taking selfies and posting them. The last one had a caption. "The Paulson High football team is _____. Fill in the blank."

With only minutes to go, the score was 21–0. Kevin checked his phone. The selfie already had 20,000 likes.

"Let's get out of here," Kevin said to Kyla.

Kevin drove them to Pizza Express. The place would soon be packed. They sat at a table in the center of the room. Everyone would be sure to see them.

"That shirt looks really good on you, Kev," Kyla said.

"Thanks, babe." Kevin stared at his phone. He hadn't seen two guys coming his way.

Both wore all black. Hoodies, jeans, and sneakers.

One held a box. That wouldn't surprise Kevin. It was common for fans to bring him gifts.

Without missing a beat, Kevin looked up and smiled. He was always on. "What's up?"

"Kevin Sanders?" one guy said.

There was no time to answer. Something came flying toward him. He could only sit there and take whatever it was.

Splat!

Kevin touched his face. His fingers felt something cold. It was some kind of sticky goo. He pulled back his hand. Whipped cream! He could taste the flavor of banana.

The ultimate prankster had just been pranked.

"I'm Brad Harris," the guy said. "Harris as in Mr. Harris. The sub you made fun of. Now who's the butt of the joke?"

Kevin blinked through the goo. He started to wipe it from his eyes.

"Why are you just sitting there?" Brad said. "Get up and fight. Or are you afraid?"

Everyone in the place had gotten quiet. All eyes were on Kevin. Brad's friend was recording the whole thing. Other people also held up their phones.

"Embarrassed? How does it feel?" Brad asked. "Just wait till I post the video."

A worker came up to the table. "Leave," she said to Brad. "Or I'll call the police."

Brad leaned toward Kevin. "Where are your followers now?" He and his friend laughed as they left.

A video like this could ruin Kevin's career. Maybe his agent could help. Kevin texted Ron. "Call me. Now!"

Chapter 5

BAD PUBLICITY

Kevin drove Kyla home. "Check YouTube," he told her. As he pulled into the driveway, his phone buzzed. It was his agent. Kevin told him what happened.

"Look, Kev," Ron said. "I get it. You feel like a jerk. But YouTube is not going to block that video."

"Why? I bring in a lot of traffic."

"So do a lot of other people. They don't block content for you. Not for anyone. And even if you could get them to do it? Why would you want to?" Ron laughed. "There's no such thing as bad publicity."

"I didn't say the guy could film me."

"Listen to yourself. You want to play pranks on people. But you don't want them played on you."

"I gotta go." Kevin ended the call. He looked over at Kyla. She was looking at her phone and laughing.

"You have to admit," she said. "It is kind of funny."

"Really? You think that's funny? What is wrong with you people?"

Later that night, Kevin was sitting with his parents. They were talking business.

Kevin's dad looked up from his laptop. "There are a lot of cafes in town. Have you reached out to any?"

"I'm working on a list now," his mom said. "I plan to make some calls tomorrow."

"What are you guys talking about?" Kevin asked.

"How to cash in on this pie thing," Kevin's dad said. "Oh! I just got it. Something with a bakery. It's a win-win."

Kevin didn't know what to say.

His dad smiled. "No deal is a bad deal. Isn't that what your agent says?"

"Something like that."

♕

The time was 3:47 a.m. Kevin lay staring at the clock. He hadn't yet watched Brad's video. Maybe it went away overnight.

Why had Brad reacted that way? No one had ever thought Kevin's pranks were real. In his mind, they were having fun too. No one got hurt. Not seriously.

Chapter 6

Insta-Shame

anders got what he deserves!"

"Love this vid!"

"LMAO!"

Three million people had seen the video. There were over 100,000 comments. Most were bad. Kevin did not want to know. But he couldn't *not* know. Finally he hit play.

First was the close-up of Kevin's face. His lips were oddly twisted. A filter had made them bright red. The rest was in slow motion. His eyes opened wide. Shoulders hunched as he braced. *Smack!* His head moved back and bobbed. Splatters of neon lime whipped cream went flying. Pieces of pie stuck to his face. He scraped it away and licked his finger.

That wasn't the end. There was a quick rewind. And

the video started again. All Kevin could think was freak show. He looked like some kind of crazed clown.

They can't do this to me! I'm Kevin Sanders!

Kevin had to pull it together. He had a meet and greet at View U. It was like See It Live but smaller. The whole pie thing would be dead by then.

When he arrived, a few girls came up to him. They wanted selfies. This made him relax a little.

Just as I thought. Nothing lasts online. Nothing stupid. He pulled a girl from the crowd. "Let's do this."

The girl was thrilled. She held out her phone. Kevin leaned over. He pressed his head to hers. Then he flashed a big smile.

"Pie!" someone yelled.

Without thinking, Kevin ducked. The pie flew over his head. It hit the wall and stuck there. After a few seconds, it slid toward the floor. Kevin stood and looked around. A sea of faces stared back. Did one of them do it? Then he saw the girl who took the selfie. Had she set him up?

"Hey, Kev." It was Chase. He was with another guy. The two of them were laughing.

"What the—" Kevin started to say. "The pie just now. Did you do that?"

"We were just having some fun. You know Alex, don't you?"

"Yeah," Kevin said. He recognized the guy from his trick-bike videos.

"Sup?" Alex said.

"Look, I'm working right now. I'll talk to you later." Kevin walked into the crowd. But he could still hear Chase.

"That pie thing really shook him up."

Kevin fought the urge to turn around. He wanted to say that Chase was wrong. But that would be a lie. Kevin *was* shook up.

Chapter 7

SAVING FACE

That Sunday, Kevin did a photo shoot. It was for a brand of watches. Afterward, he texted Kyla. He reminded her about dinner. "Pick U up in 30."

"Can't wait!" she texted.

As Kevin left the set, something made him stop. He looked back. A guy from the crew was on a laptop. There was a meme on the screen. It was Kevin with pie on his face. He moved closer to read the caption. "Can't take what he dishes out."

Kevin's head was spinning. Did the watch company know about this? He could be fired. Word would get around. It would ruin everything.

Until now, Kevin had tried to forget the pie prank. But it wasn't going away. Brad Harris had pushed Kevin too far. He texted Chase. "Need help with a revenge prank."

Kevin and Chase met the next day. They were at a fast food place.

"What's the plan?" Chase asked.

"I need someone to scare Brad Harris. Know anyone who will do it?"

"Yeah. For a price."

"A shout-out on social media?"

"No. Cash only."

♔

Kevin never came to the West Hills Mall. It was a little out of his way. But he'd heard that Brad would be here.

Now he peered out from behind a tall potted plant. A ball cap was pulled down over his eyes. He was trying to keep a low profile. That wasn't easy for him. He was so well known. But today the mall was packed. That would help him blend in.

Then Kevin saw him. Brad was with his girlfriend. They sat at a table inside the food court. Once Chase's friend got here, the prank would begin.

Kevin looked around. A guy was coming his way. He wore a tight black T-shirt. His muscles bulged through the thin material. As he got closer, Kevin looked at him. He lifted up the brim of his cap. The guy stopped.

"Kevin Sanders," he said.

"Luke?"

"Yeah, man. Love your pranks."

"Thanks," Kevin said. He nodded toward the food court. "That's him. The guy with the red jacket."

Luke looked over at Brad. "You want me to scare him. But not hurt him."

"Right. But take it as far as you can."

Luke headed to the food court. Kevin started filming. The scene was of Brad and his girlfriend. They were talking and laughing. Luke stopped at the table. Brad looked up. He had a smile on his face. Luke was speaking.

After a few seconds, Brad stopped smiling. He started to get up. That's when Luke pushed him down. Kevin moved the camera to Brad's girlfriend. She looked upset. Then he panned around the food court. People just watched.

The camera was back on Brad. He said something to his girlfriend. Then he stood and walked away. As he left the food court, he stumbled.

That's when Luke grabbed him. He drew back his fist. Kevin zoomed in on Brad's face. His eyes were wide with fear. It looked like he was about to cry. This was Kevin's cue.

Still filming, he walked toward Luke and Brad. The

camera was focused on Brad's face. Then suddenly he wasn't in the shot.

Kevin lowered the phone. He saw Brad lying on the ground. Then he looked at Luke. "Did you push him down?"

Chapter 8

REVENGE

The guy fell," Luke said. "Look. He's shaking."

"I have to get a shot of it!" Before Kevin could film, a guard headed their way. "Let's get out of here," he said. They left the mall.

Outside, Kevin was watching the video back. "You had him so scared, he was shaking."

"It wasn't like that," Luke said. "He fell. Then he started shaking. It could have been a seizure."

"What do you mean?"

"My brother has them. It can happen when you have epilepsy. Maybe you shouldn't post that."

"Don't worry about it. Here's your money."

Who was this loser to tell Kevin not to do something? Luke had been the one to practically scare a kid to death. It didn't matter. Kevin had what he needed.

♛

Kevin was on his computer when Kyla called. He told her about the video. "Brad was scared out of his mind. It was seriously funny."

"Listen, babe. Maybe you shouldn't post it."

The video was uploading to YouTube. "Why not?" Kevin said. "He did it to me."

"It's not the same thing. What if Brad has a disability? It will look like you're making fun of him. That's not cool."

"He started this." As Kevin said the words, he knew how it sounded. But revenge was so close.

Kyla was silent. She didn't like to argue with him. Deep down he had to know this was wrong. And he'd do the right thing. At least she hoped so.

Before uploading, He typed in a title. "Revenge Is Sweet."

It was after 1:00 a.m. Kevin couldn't sleep. He checked how the video was doing. YouTube had put it on the front page. There were over one million views.

Kevin felt good. It was the first time since the pie prank. *Nobody messes with Kevin Sanders.*

Too bad no one was around. Kevin started to text Kyla. But he stopped. It was late. And she wouldn't approve anyway. He'd tell his parents later. They would be pleased.

Chapter 9

BACKFIRED

Kevin woke Monday to his phone buzzing. He looked at the screen. *Oh crap! The interview.* He'd forgotten about it.

What was her name? Kevin looked at his notes. *Carly. Social media expert.* Carly had a weekly podcast. She gave advice on how to be instafamous. Her show had a great title. "Don't Ask Me." The advice must have been good. Her show had millions of viewers.

"All set?" Carly asked.

"Shoot," Kevin said.

He was tired. But he knew how to turn it on. And he was a good talker. Besides, the questions were always the same. How did you get started? Who inspired you? What's your best prank? What advice do you have? This interview was like that.

Kevin checked the time. It was almost over.

"One more thing," Carly said. "It's about your latest video. Did you think so many people would hate it?"

"Huh?" What was she saying? Kevin hadn't checked YouTube lately.

"Well … um ..." Kevin grabbed his laptop. He opened YouTube.

"You had to see it coming," she said.

A new video was up. He read the title. "What Sanders Didn't Show You." Kevin clicked on it. He nearly dropped the phone.

"I'm sorry," he said to Carly. "I need to end this."

The video started with Brad on the ground. His arms and legs made jerking motions. It looked like he couldn't breathe. His girlfriend was beside him. People crowded around. Some shouted for help. Then the camera panned to Kevin. He was leaving the mall.

Kevin called Ron. He'd seen the video. "What should I do?" Kevin asked. "Post an apology?"

"Do nothing," Ron said. "Not right now."

"How can you be so calm? People think I hurt that kid. They think he has a disability. I need to do something."

"And lose everything you've built? All the buzz and traffic? Go ahead. But this will all turn around. Then you'll have nothing. Nada."

It was ten o'clock when Kevin got to school. He told the office he'd overslept.

"R U OK?" Kyla texted him.

"Yeah, why?"

"Check IG."

Kevin's feed was filled with memes. One showed Brad. He was on the ground. There was a caption too. "Kevin Sanders did this!" He scanned the comments. One caught his eye.

"Sanders disses the disabled! #wasteofspace."

Kevin felt sick. At lunch, he sat with Adam and Nick. He'd just checked Instagram.

"Hey, guys. I'm down 2,000. Do you think it will hit zero?"

The two kept talking. It was as if he wasn't there.

On his way home, he called Ron. "Am I still on for True Stars?"

The deal was with Omni Sneakers. Kevin was set to do a meet and greet. It paid $6,000.

"No. I killed it. They lowered their offer at the last minute. It was an insult. Your parents said you wanted time off," Ron said. "Take this as a good thing."

"Yeah," Kevin said. But he knew it wasn't good.

He texted Kyla. "Can't meet tonight. See U tomorrow."

Chapter 10

Going Nowhere

It was Tuesday after school. Kevin and Kyla were meeting for coffee. Kevin was outside the shop waiting. He was on his phone when she pulled up.

"Hi," she said as she got out of the car.

Kevin didn't say anything. He was still staring at his phone. She walked past him and went inside. Kevin followed. They sat at a table in the back.

"I know you're bummed," Kyla said. "So a few people are hating on you. Who cares? It won't last."

"Who cares?" Anger welled up inside him. "This is my career. My life."

"What about Brad?" Kyla asked. "He's the one who got hurt. Have you reached out to him? No."

"He started this!"

"Stop saying that. You sound like a spoiled brat. All you care about is your fame."

"Maybe if you had more followers, you'd get it."

They sat in silence for a few minutes. Then Kevin got up. "I'll be right back." He headed for the bathroom.

In the hallway, two girls came up to him. They stood on either side. One of the girls held up her phone. They leaned in for a selfie.

"Perfect!" the other one said.

Kevin stepped out from between them. He turned to thank them for being fans. Even in a bad mood, he could be nice. That's when he saw it. One girl had been holding a pie.

He went back to the table and sat down. "Everyone hates me," he said.

Kyla rolled her eyes. "No wonder Bryan stopped pranking with you."

"What do you mean?" He kept scrolling through his phone.

"I think he knew the truth about fame. Your followers only love you when you're on top."

"You're saying I'm not on top? My followers don't love me?" It hurt Kevin to hear it.

"You're more than your fame, Kev. You're a great guy."

Kevin hadn't heard her. He'd gotten a text from Ron. It was more bad news.

"Show List is off. Motto Clothing pulled out."

His mind was racing. It was another event where Kevin Sanders wouldn't be seen. Unless he went on his own.

Kevin spent the rest of the week planning. He'd go to Show List, and his fans would be happy.

♛

It was Saturday. Kevin drove to the fairgrounds. Show List was being held in one of the big halls. He parked and walked up to the entrance. There was a long line of people waiting to get in.

A guy Kevin knew was working the door. His name was Jay.

"What's up, Kev?" Jay said.

"Hey, Jay."

"How have you been?"

"Good," Kevin lied.

A man brushed past Kevin. He wore an ID badge. It said "All Access." Jay opened the door for him, and he went inside.

"You've got a pass?" Jay asked Kevin.

"Um, no," Kevin said.

"No pass?"

This had been a bad idea. It was embarrassing to be questioned like this.

Jay smiled. "No pass. No problem." He handed Kevin a pass. It was gold with the letters *VIP*.

"Only top status for my man Kevin Sanders."

Kevin shook Jay's hand and hurried inside. The first thing he saw was the Motto booth. It was huge. They hadn't pulled out of Show List. The company had pulled out of working with Kevin. It felt like a punch in the gut. Suddenly he felt like all eyes were on him. The look on their faces was the same. Disgust.

A crowd of people was coming. As they passed, Kevin saw Chase. Their eyes met for a second. Then Chase walked right by. He didn't even say hi. It was like Kevin was poison.

Chapter 11

DROPPED

He should have called by now," Kevin said.

He and his parents were waiting to hear from Ron. *Please let it be about a job,* Kevin thought. This could all turn around. Even Ron thought so at one point.

Finally Ron called. His face came up on the computer screen. He got right to the point.

"This Brad thing has gotten too big. It's hard to get Kevin work."

Kevin knew what was coming. Ron was dropping him. He glanced at his parents. They looked shocked.

"You've seen the numbers," Ron said. "Your followers are way down."

"You can't drop him," Kevin's dad said. "This can be fixed. Kevin can post an apology."

This plea seemed weak to Kevin. His dad wasn't thinking about him. He was thinking about the money.

"It's too late for that," Ron said.

"Too late?" Kevin said. "I wanted to take it down a long time ago. You said not to."

"Let's stay in touch," Ron said. "Kevin, keep thinking up new pranks. Get people excited again. Your followers may come back."

Brand. Likes. Followers. They'd never been a problem for Kevin. Now his world was falling apart. He needed some air. A walk would help him think.

First he put on sunglasses and a cap. Before he'd done this to keep fans from swarming him. Now it was to hide from his haters.

Where was he going? Nowhere. He just walked. Out of habit, he checked his social media accounts. He'd lost even more followers. It was all because of a prank. A really stupid prank. There was nothing he could do. He felt defeated.

What if he just let go of it all? What would it feel like? He took a long breath. Then he closed the apps. After that, he turned off his phone. What a surprise. He felt relief.

What did it mean to be instafamous anyway? Looking perfect? That wasn't real. Besides the money, there was nothing meaningful about it. The world wasn't a better place because of it.

The next day Kevin still hadn't turned his phone on.

"It's weird talking to you on a landline," Kyla said. "What happened to your phone?"

"It broke." That wasn't true. He was too scared to turn it back on.

Chapter 12

REWIND

After Kevin studied, he went for a walk. He hadn't planned to go to Bryan's. But that's where he ended up.

As young boys, the two hung out here. Kevin and his parents had lived in a tiny apartment at the time. Bryan's parents had a big backyard with a pool. There was room to run and play. They could be as loud as they wanted. Some of their first pranks started right here.

As teens they got into video games. That led them to social media. Soon they got popular doing pranks. They were always in YouTube's top ten. Then Bryan lost his nerve. He couldn't do pranks anymore.

"Get over it!" Kevin had yelled. But it wasn't that simple.

After that they talked less and less. And then not at all. Being at different high schools didn't help.

Kevin crossed the street. He was nervous, but he stepped up to the door and knocked.

Bryan's mom opened the door. "Kevin!" she cried. There was a big smile on her face.

"Hi, Mrs. Lowe." He gave her a hug.

Kevin had always liked Bryan's parents. They were like a second mom and dad. Sometimes he wished his own parents were like them. Not caught up in fame.

Both of Bryan's parents worked. Mrs. Lowe was an author. She also homeschooled Bryan when his fear of going places got too bad. His dad was a chef at a top restaurant. But work never got in the way of family.

"Let me get Bryan," she said.

As she turned, Bryan came up behind her.

"Hey, Bry!" Kevin said.

Bryan smiled. "Been a while."

They sat in the living room.

"I heard what people are saying about you," Bryan said.

"So you're back on social media?"

"No. My little sister told me. What are you going to do? I know how much it means to you."

"My little problems aren't important. Besides, I'm done," Kevin said. "I even turned my phone off." He held it up to show his friend.

Bryan laughed. "There's no way. You were on that thing 24/7."

They both got quiet. After a minute, Kevin started to speak. "Hey, Bry. I'm really sorry about—"

"Dude, don't get all serious on me."

"I just—"

"It's cool. I couldn't do social media anymore. You had to go on. There was too much to lose."

"Are you okay now?"

"The meds help. I don't care so much about getting people's approval. And I'm not as worried all the time."

On his way home, Kevin reached for his phone. He started to turn it on. A week ago he would have already posted pics of himself and Bryan. Instead, he just kept walking.

Two hours later, he was back on Instagram. It was like a bad accident. He had to look. Most comments were negative.

"Who picks on a person with a disability?"

"So low even for Kevin Sanders."

"This guy is garbage."

Kevin was about to close Instagram. That's when he saw an ad. It was for Talent Icon. It was the biggest social media event of the year. Last year it was held in another state. A company flew him there. They paid for everything. This year it was in California. And he had not been invited.

Kevin went to talk to his parents. "I've been thinking," he said. "I want to tell Brad that I'm sorry."

His dad looked up. "You mean make a video."

"That's a great idea," his mom said.

His dad started to make plans. "He can do it live on YouTube."

His mom was nodding. "People love drama like that."

"Stop!" Kevin said. "I want to tell Brad in person. It's not for ratings. It's the right thing to do."

His parents were staring at him.

"You know how it works," his dad said. "This thing with Harris will get old. You need to do something online. Or it will all go away. Is that what you want?"

"Yes!" Kevin said. "I'm sick of people hating on me. No one knows the real story. Why I did what I did. Yeah, my online status matters. But I'm not just a brand. I care about people. And this is no joke."

Followers

Kyla and Kevin were at the mall. They were walking through a store. "You're so quiet," Kevin said. "What's wrong?"

"I was just thinking," Kyla said. "You have millions of followers. That must be so cool. But they're not real friends. Don't you miss that? And I know what you're going to say. I'm just jealous."

"Well, aren't you?" Kevin asked. He smiled.

"No," Kyla said. "Be serious for a second."

"I guess I think of my followers as friends. We have our own little world. We're in it together."

"What if you never get them back? Will you be okay with that?"

Kevin noticed two girls. They were looking in his direction. Their phones were aimed at him.

Kyla had seen them too. "What are you thinking?" she asked.

He didn't answer her.

"You might as well deal with it," she said. "Before things go too far."

He knew Kyla was right. "Hey, ladies," he called out.

"You're Kevin Sanders," one of them said.

"I figured that's why you were filming me."

"I'm Tara. This is Chloe. Can we take a selfie with you?"

"Sure," Kevin said. He stepped between them.

Chloe reached into her shopping bag. She pulled out a pie. "Would you mind holding this?"

"I'd rather not," he said. "That prank is old. It's something I'm not proud of."

"Oh, sorry," Tara said. "We didn't mean—"

"It's okay." Kevin wasn't mad at the girls. He knew they didn't mean any harm. They were just trying to build their brand. The photos would drive some traffic to their page.

The girls got their selfies. Then Tara asked if they could interview him. "We're making a show for YouTube. You'd be our first online celebrity."

"Cool," he said.

He was surprised by the questions. They didn't ask about Brad Harris. Instead, they focused on his early career. They asked him what it was like to work with Bryan Lowe. Their old shows were still on YouTube. The pranks were still funny.

It felt good to talk about it. Those were great times. Kevin would be seeing Bryan later that day. He'd have to tell him.

Chapter 14

SORRY

I'm glad you came over," Bryan said. "It's good to hang out again. Are your basketball skills any better?"

Kevin went for the shot. Bryan grabbed the ball mid-air and slammed it.

"You've still got it!" Kevin said. "You should play with Kyla sometime. She'd kick your butt."

Bryan loved basketball. He'd once been on his high school's team. But then he and Kevin started getting famous. Doing pranks took up all their time. When Bryan's anxiety got bad, he quit everything. Basketball included.

Kevin wanted to talk about it. There had been chances. The two had gotten together a few times. But somehow the topic was always Kevin. What he was going through.

Bryan passed Kevin the ball. "How's it going with Instagram?"

"It's not," Kevin said. He took a shot and missed.

"You never were good at sports." Bryan smiled. "Not like you were at being online. Remember all those events we'd do? You were a beast. For me, it was such hard work. There was never a break. I was afraid I couldn't keep up. Then it finally happened."

"I thought you were on board. Why didn't you say something? We could have slowed down."

"How? We were so tied to that world. And to each other. If we slowed down, we would have been out. I couldn't let you fail because of me. Besides, I'd always been half of Lowe and Lower. Who was I without that?"

Bryan picked up the ball and dribbled it. "Then there was that first panic attack. It decided things for me. I thought I'd feel better. Instead, I questioned everything. Who I was. What my life was about. In some ways, I wished I could be back in your world. But I was stuck. No way back. And no way forward."

"I'm sorry, Bry. I didn't get it."

♕

One apology down. One to go.

Kevin was at Southland Park to meet Brad. The plan was for just the two of them to meet. But Mr. Harris was there too. What would Kevin say to the sub he made fun of?

Mr. Harris scowled as Kevin walked up to them.

"Hey, Brad," Kevin said. Then he looked at Mr. Harris. "I'm sorry, sir, for the prank I pulled on you. I don't expect you to forgive me."

"I'm only here to support my son," he said.

Kevin looked at Brad. "Can we talk alone?"

They stepped away from Mr. Harris.

"Look," Kevin said. "I'm sorry about what happened. I never should've done that to your dad. It was messed up."

"It would have been funny if it wasn't my dad. You know, I used to follow you. But then I just wanted to teach you a lesson."

"But what I did to you was even—" Kevin stopped talking. Brad was smiling. "I'm being serious," he said. "What I did was wrong."

"I know. But I was wrong too."

"Why? What did you do besides the pie?"

"Look, dude. The seizure wasn't real. I faked it. It was the only way to get that guy to back off. Then I saw you talking to him. That's when I knew. You were behind the whole thing. It was too good to pass up. I turned your prank around. The great Kevin Sanders wasn't so great anymore."

This was a lot for Kevin to take in. He thought about the negative posts and everything he'd lost. Followers.

Product deals. His agent. It was all because of something fake. It never had to happen.

Maybe he should have been angry. But all he felt was relief. People thought he was a monster. But there were two sides.

"No one else knows you faked it?" Kevin asked.

"No. I guess I wouldn't blame you if you said something."

"I'm not going to. And I'm still sorry. I don't care if you faked it or not."

"I do have epilepsy," Brad said. "But I haven't had a seizure in years. It wasn't cool to lie about it."

"We both messed up," Kevin said.

Chapter 15

Are You Pranking Me?

"So we talked and it's all good. You can stop hating on him."

That was the end of an Instagram post. It was from Brad Harris to his followers. He was letting them know that Kevin was cool. The current number of likes was over 400,000.

Kevin had watched it twice. Brad didn't admit he messed up. He didn't say the seizure was fake. But that was okay. Kevin got it. Brad didn't get popular by being Kevin's friend. The truth might have made his followers mad. They could turn on him.

Of all the comments, most were negative. But some were actually good.

"Kevin Sanders is legit."

"It takes a big person to say they're sorry."

Kevin closed the app and started his homework. It was almost six o'clock when he got a call. The number wasn't familiar.

"Hey, Kev."

It was Bryan. "Dude, what's up?" This was a big deal. Bryan never called. For a long time, he kept his phone off. Then he got rid of it. He must have gotten a new one.

"Not much. My sister showed me Brad's post. I think it's great that you guys talked."

"Yeah." He started to tell Bryan the real story. But he stopped. All that negative stuff was a waste of time.

The two talked about what they had going on. Kevin was still off social media. Bryan was thinking about going somewhere. It would be a place close by, like the grocery store.

"Kyla and I are going out to eat later. You should come." It had been more of a question. Kevin knew the answer would be no. But he wanted to make it an option. One of these days Bryan would say yes.

"Oh, well, no. Not tonight. Maybe next time."

"You got it," Kevin said. "Hey, remember Native? The clothing company. They used to send us shirts?"

"I remember," Bryan said. "I didn't like their earlier styles. But some of the newer designs are cool."

"They sent me a shirt. I think I'll wear it tonight. I'll send you a picture."

"Post it on Instagram too. I might even comment."

Kevin finished getting dressed and went downstairs. He was surprised to see his parents watching TV. For once they weren't on their devices.

"I'm going to Kyla's," Kevin said. He went to the door. Then he turned to look at his parents. "Are you guys okay? I mean with me just wanting to be myself?"

His mom and dad looked at each other.

"Well," his dad said. "The dream was to quit working early. While we're still sort of young. Now we'll just have to go get real jobs."

Kevin knew that his dad was only half joking.

"Sure, we've gotten used to the money. But this is your life. You have to do what's right for you."

"If you could just do it online?" his mom said.

Kevin's eyes got wide.

"I'm kidding!" she said. "Go on. We'll talk later."

Real Time

The restaurant Kyla chose was packed. The only open table was on the patio. But the fall air was still warm, so they took it.

After a few minutes of talking and laughing, Kevin got serious. "I made such a mess of things," he said. "A lot of girls wouldn't have stuck around."

"That's why I'm awesome," Kyla said. Then she smiled. "You know I'll always tell you the truth. Even when you don't want to hear it. I'm not some random follower. Sometimes you have a big ego. It turns you into a jerk. This experience has been good for you in a way. You're more like the Kevin I first knew."

"I just …"

Kevin and Kyla had always been able to talk to each

other. Kevin was never afraid to show his feelings. But right now, what could he say? "You're great." "Thanks for loving me." It wasn't enough. But he trusted her to get it.

Now Kyla was leaning forward. She looked into Kevin's eyes.

"You always knew the real me. Even when I didn't," Kevin said.

He saw the look in her eyes. She got it. Kevin didn't need to say a bunch of words.

Kyla continued to look at him. She took his hand. "What you did was lame. But it wasn't the worst thing in the world. No one died."

This was what he needed to hear. She didn't think he was a bad person.

"You look really good in that shirt," she said. "Green is a good color on you." She held up her phone.

"Hold on. Let me fix my hair." He brushed it back from his eyes. "Here, I'll hold up this soda."

It was too late. She had taken the picture. It was him in the moment. She looked at the photo. "Wow. I'm a pretty good photographer."

"Let me see." He took the phone. The photo was simple. He wasn't in some awkward pose. There was no slick filter to make his features pop. It just looked like him.

"We have to send this to Bryan. I promised I would."

Kevin typed a message. It read, "Hey, Lowe. Like the shirt?" He texted the picture. Then he sent it to himself.

"Are you going to post it?" Kyla asked.

"Yeah. The Insta-world needs a new picture of me."

♔

A day after it posted, Kyla's photo of Kevin had over 200,000 likes. Kevin had gained followers. On Instagram and his YouTube channel. He wondered if his parents knew about it. When he went downstairs, they were waiting for him.

"Sit down," his dad said.

"Why?" Kevin asked. "What did I do now?"

"We got a call from Native clothing," his dad said. "It's about that picture you posted. You're wearing their shirt."

"Yeah? Let me guess. They want me to take it down. It's bad for their brand."

"Hardly," his mom said. "That photo has gone viral for them."

He felt his heart beat a little faster. This was good news. The Insta-world had finally shifted. Kevin Sanders was no longer a joke.

"Native's CEO called with an offer," his dad said.

"Oh yeah?" Kevin asked. He was trying to play it cool.

"Wait before you say anything. It's not great. But it's

a chance to be at Talent Icon. Native will pay you $1,500 to represent them."

Kevin was silent.

"I know," his dad said. "You used to get three times that amount. But remember. That was with a huge fan base and an agent."

"Can I think about it?" Kevin asked.

"I wouldn't wait too long," his mom said. "Why not do this? See if you can build a relationship. Once your brand is back on top, we'll ask for more money."

"I'm just not sure I want to do it," he said.

Chapter 17

REBOUND

Why wouldn't you do it?" Bryan asked. Kevin and Bryan were shooting hoops at Bryan's house. "You used to love going to Talent Icon." Bryan put the ball up. It bounced off the rim.

Kevin grabbed it. He dribbled toward the hoop and made a one-handed shot. "One minute I want to do it," Kevin said. "The next minute I don't. I mean, everyone hated me. And now suddenly they love me again?" He shook his head. "It just seems kind of lame."

"It makes sense to me. They hated you because they loved you so much."

"That's too deep for me, man."

"You were their hero. Then you let them down. So they found a new hero. That was Brad. Now Brad is cool with you. Then what? You're the hero again."

"I guess. It seems kind of sick."

"Ya think?" Bryan said. "Sorry, but none of it's real. Those people don't really know you. They just think they do."

"Would you come?" Kevin asked.

Bryan laughed. "To Talent Icon?"

Kevin had a serious look on his face.

"Come on, dude. You know the answer to that. I'm just saying. If you want to do it, you should." He tossed Kevin the ball. "But this time, do it on your terms."

♕

Dave Morris was on speakerphone. The CEO of Native Clothing sounded excited. Kevin and his parents were listening.

"Kevin, you really got our attention. That photo of you in our shirt went crazy on social media. In fact, when people search Native, your picture comes up."

"Cool," Kevin said.

"Our Instagram has blown up because of you. It just makes sense that you be in our booth at Talent Icon. We are so psyched to have you represent us."

"Thank you," Kevin said.

"Dave," Kevin's dad said. "About the appearance. Kevin has a few points he'd like to go over."

"Of course. Go ahead, Kevin."

"Hey, Dave," Kevin said. "First off, thank you for this

chance you're offering me. I'm totally down for it. There are just a few things. I want to make sure you're okay with it."

"Sure, Kevin. Let's hear it," Dave said.

"I don't want to do any pranks. That's not my focus right now. I just want to be myself. I'm only agreeing to work the booth. Anything beyond that we'll discuss. Last, you get me for three hours."

There was a pause on the other end of the phone. Kevin and his parents looked at each other. Finally Dave spoke. "Kevin, I accept your terms. You have nothing to worry about. Native wants you to be you."

After the call ended, Kevin texted Bryan. "Going to Talent Icon! My terms!"

Bryan texted back a thumbs-up.

Chapter 18

TALENT ICON

It was a few days later. Kevin and Kyla were headed to San Diego. Kevin drove in silence.

"Are you okay?" Kyla finally said.

"Sorry," he said. "I don't mean to shut you out."

"It's not that. I know you're thinking about the event."

It was like Kyla had read his mind. His stomach was in knots. Every scene played out in his head. No one noticed him. Everyone noticed him. Native's booth was empty. Maybe people would laugh at him. They'd throw pies. There would be a blitz of negative posts.

"Here's what I don't get," Kyla said. "Why do you want to go through this? Do you miss the fame that much? I've never had it. Maybe I'd want it back too if I lost it."

"I'm not sure what I want. I just feel like I need to be there."

"Are you afraid?"

"What do you mean?"

"That if you don't go, you'll end up like Bryan."

Kevin looked over at Kyla.

"Like you'll be too scared to do anything," she said.

"No. I think that would have happened to Bryan anyway. He was living with fear for a long time. For me, it was one bad experience. I don't want to pass things up because of it."

The event was held in two buildings. Lines of people waited to get inside. Hall A was where the biggest stars were. They were doing a meet and greet with fans. Kevin and Kyla went to Hall B. That's where the Native booth was.

The hall was packed. People were elbow to elbow. Once in a while there would be screams. Fans had seen an online star.

Kevin and Kyla made their way across the room. They passed rows of booths. Every type of business was there. Clothing. Movies. Books.

All the noise had made Kevin dizzy. So far, no one had seemed to notice him. But then, he wasn't trying to get attention. Just ahead, he saw a huge crowd. They were in front of a booth. It was Native Clothing. This was a good sign.

A few people were inside the booth working. One man stood out. He was older. His hair was short and spiky.

"Kevin!" the man called out. He walked up to Kevin. They shook hands. "Dave Morris, CEO of Native."

"Hi," Kevin said. "This is my girlfriend."

Dave shook Kyla's hand. Then he smiled at Kevin. "What do you think of this crowd? You've got a big following."

At that moment, Kevin knew it would be okay. No matter what happened today, he was clear on one thing. He knew who he was.

It didn't matter why people were here to see him. Maybe they loved the old Kevin. Or they were curious to see what happened to him. Many could have been new fans. They'd seen the photo Kyla took. Just a normal guy wearing a green shirt.

"Well," Kevin said. "I guess it's time." He walked into the booth. There was a rush of excitement. People gathered around.

"Kevin Sanders!" they called out.

"Love everything you do!" someone shouted.

A single voice called out, "Selfie!"

Then others joined in. "Selfie!"

Something turned on inside him. It was like a light switch. Kevin loved being in front of a crowd. He loved everything about it. Talking to people. Taking selfies. Doing interviews.

When he'd gotten here, his plan was to hold back. He wouldn't share too much. It was a way to protect himself. But that wasn't him. Neither was the prankster. Kevin didn't have to be either of those people. He could make it as himself.

Chapter 19

FACING IT

Two hours had passed. There hadn't been a single pie. Nothing stupid lasted long on social media. That included pranks.

Now Kevin could admit it. Prank videos were dumb. Some were funny. But mostly they ruined people's day. Worse, they hurt people.

Someone from Native suggested that Kevin walk the floor. He could do a mobile meet and greet. Kevin looked out at the dense crowd. Then he looked at Kyla.

"It's up to you," she said. "But I'm kind of surprised. Before you were nervous just to be here."

"I know," Kevin said. "But what's there to lose? Plus Native is paying me to work the crowd."

"So you're glad you're here?"

"Yeah, I am," he said.

Kyla followed him through the crowd. Every few seconds, someone called his name. Some people filmed him with their phones. Others asked for selfies.

"Kevvy," someone called. "Can I get a pic?"

OMG. It was Chase. The last time Kevin saw him was at Show List. Chase had totally dissed him. Just as he came in for a hug, Kevin stepped back. He put his arm around Kyla.

"Hey, Kyla," Chase said.

She gave a quick motion with her head.

"What's up, bro?" Chase said.

"Not much. Just working," Kevin said.

"Native? Really?" Chase asked. "What's that like? You can tell me the truth. I won't say anything."

In the past, they both thought Native Clothing was a joke. Only nine-year-olds wore their stuff.

"The company is great. They hired me, didn't they? Do you like my shirt? It's part of their newest line. Dope, right? Maybe I can get you one."

"Uh, yeah. Sure," Chase said. "It sounds like things are going good. Even after everything that happened. The way your fans turned on you. That was so messed up. I never believed what they were saying. Whenever I had an interview, I stood up for you."

"Funny," Kyla piped up. "We never saw any of that."

Chase looked at her. Kevin just smiled. It was funny to see Chase get called out on his crap.

"Hey, Chase. You should watch out. What happened to me? It could happen to you too."

"I hope not," Chase said. "Do you want to do a prank?"

"Nah. I'm over that. I want to do something that helps people."

Chapter 20

Owning It

Talent Icon had been a success. Native Clothing was excited to work with Kevin. The CEO said he wanted to make another deal.

Kevin and Kyla had left the center. They were walking to Kevin's car. The night air was cold. Kevin pulled Kyla close to him to warm her.

"What do you want to do?" she asked. "Head home?"

"Yeah. The traffic is pretty bad. It'll take a while."

They got into the car. He started the engine. Then he looked at her. "You know what? I really want to see Bryan."

"Do you think that's a good idea?"

Kevin pulled out of the parking space. He drove slowly through the crowd.

"You don't want to?" he asked.

"It's not that. I just wonder if Bryan's ready. He's fine seeing just you. I'm not sure—"

"I don't think he'd mind a quick visit."

They drove away from the convention center. Traffic was slow.

Kyla squeezed Kevin's hand. "What about you?" she asked. "Are you okay?"

Kevin stared out the front window. His eyes were focused on the line of cars ahead. They'd go for a few seconds, then come to a sudden halt. It was like that for miles.

"I feel like part of me died."

Kyla laughed. "That's deep," she said. "You should post it."

"I know, right? But it's true. People only knew one side of me. The famous side. Maybe I will post something. It might help other people." He looked at her.

"What?" she said. "What are you thinking now?"

"We should do something together," Kevin said. "Kev and Kyla."

"What would our show be about?"

"Something positive. How to use social media to make a difference."

"I like it," she said.

"Let's talk to Bryan about it. He has good ideas."

Kevin slammed on the brakes. Traffic had come to a sudden stop again.

"I almost forgot," Kyla said. "I have something for you." She reached into her coat pocket. "Here." She handed a note to Kevin.

"What's this?"

"Read it."

Kevin opened the note. It was from his parents. They wanted him to know how proud they were. Whatever Kevin wanted to do was okay with them. They just wanted him to be happy.

He looked at Kyla. "They could have just texted me."

"I think they wanted to make it personal. Like you did with Brad. Some things are better in person. Besides, I know it means a lot to you."

"Keep telling me the truth," he said. "Even when I don't like it."

"Okay. I'll tell you the truth right now. I love the real Kevin Sanders." She had drawn $K + K$ on the frosty window. There was a heart around it.

Traffic was moving again. Kyla was on Instagram. "You're trending," she said.

Kevin looked over. It was a photo of him. He was wearing the green Native shirt. The Insta-world had met the real Kevin Sanders. "How many likes?" he asked.

WANT TO KEEP READING?

9781680214796

Turn the page for a sneak peek
at another book in the Monarch
Jungle series.

Chapter 1

KILLING IT

Yeah!" Alden shouted. He sat at a computer. Fingers of one hand tapped the keyboard. The other hand moved the mouse. His eyes darted around the screen.

A young woman sat next to him. "No!" she shouted back.

They were talking to each other through headsets.

"Bad move," Alden said.

"Dude!" she said. "Are you kidding me?"

"You shouldn't be alive!" he said.

The players were tense. There was a lot to gain. And even more to lose. Reputation. Money. Pride. This was the world of eSports. It was as big as pro football.

Alden went pro a year ago. He was a PC player. Many gamers would laugh at that. They only used consoles.

In the gaming world, it was a big debate. For Alden, it was about click speed. The PC was faster. The mouse gave good aim. That mattered in shooting games. Consoles gathered dust.

But Alden didn't make excuses. He won. His gamer name was "Black Heart." And he was in the world's top 10.

Today's game was *Dead End*. There was violence, of course. Guns. Lasers or bombs. Fist fighting at times.

Each level had two tasks. Kill the enemy and escape. There were only minutes. It took quick decisions. Fail, and your avatar died.

Alden was facing a great player. Her name was Kady Adams. "Red Ivy" was her gamer name. No one had played *Dead End* better. That would change today. It was Alden's hope anyway.

Now the two sat side by side. People looking down saw only two small dots. That didn't matter. The arena was filled with big screens. That's where the action was seen.

Black Heart was a pirate. He had long brown hair. Red Ivy's hair was crimson. She was dressed in a tank top and fatigues.

They fought. Guns went off. There were explosions. People watched in awe.

Every attack got cheers. Alden didn't hear them. His headset blocked the sound. For now, the real world didn't exist. He was in the zone.

There were five rounds altogether. So far, Alden had won two. He needed one more win. Then he would sweep the series. But Kady had never lost this game.

Today was different. Alden was feeling bold. He'd even said it to reporters. "Red Ivy is going down."

The third round started. It was set in a chemical plant. A fire was raging. They had one minute to work it out.

"I'm coming for you," Alden said into his headset. "That's right. Stay right there."

"Get off my back!" Kady yelled.

Bullets flew past Black Heart. They hit a tank of gas. Flames shot up. More tanks burst open. There was a string of explosions.

"Oh my God," Alden said.

Black Heart flew across the room. He was down. Red Ivy started shooting.

Nine, ten, eleven. Alden was counting to himself. He knew her gun had twelve bullets. One more bullet and she'd have to reload. *Twelve.*

Suddenly Black Heart stood. The crowd gasped. This was sure death. Red Ivy's gun clicked. She reached for another one. In that second, she was shot.

"Got you!" Alden shouted. The screens went black. The crowd roared. He jumped to his feet.

"Nicely done," Kady said.

The two shook hands. Then the crowd rushed in around him.

"You're the greatest gamer in the world," someone shouted.

"Nah," Alden said. He didn't like to brag. It was better to act humble. "But I did kill it today."